DR. MUNCING,
EXORCIST

BY

GORDON MACCREAGH

British Library Cataloguing-in-Publication Data
A catalogue record for this book is available from the
British Library

CONTENTS

GORDON MACCREAGH

Gordon MacCreagh was born in Perth, Indiana in 1886. Little is known about his life, other than that he was a keen traveller. He published a number of popular short stories during his lifetime, most of them in the horror genre, including 'Dr. Muncing, Exorcist' (1931), 'The Case of the Sinister Shape' (1932), 'Zimwi Crater' (1934), 'Matto Grosso Fury' (1950) and 'Projection from Epsilon' (1953). Probably MacCreagh's most popular longer work was *White Waters and Black*, an account of his explorations in the Amazon in 1923. An absurd, honest and amusing text, it is regarded by many as one of the great travel books. MacCreagh died in 1953.

DR. MUNCING, EXORCIST

The brass plate on the gate post of the trim white wicket said only: Dr. Muncing, Exorcist.

Aside from that, the house was just the same as all the others in that street—semi-detached, whitewashed, respectable. A few more brass plates announced other sober citizens with their sprinkling of doctors of medicine and one of divinity. But Dr. Muncing, Exorcist; that was suggestive of something quite different and strange.

The man who gazed reflectively out of the window at the driving rain, was, like his brass sign, vaguely suggestive, too, of something strange; of having the capacity to do something that the other sober citizens, doctors and lawyers, did not do.

He was of a little more than middle height, broad, with strong, capable-looking hands; his face was square cut, finely criss-crossed with weatherbeaten lines, tanned from much travel in far-away lands; a strong nose hung over a thin, wide mouth that closed with an extraordinary determination.

The face of a normal man of strong character. It was the eyes that conveyed that vague impression of something unusual. Deep set, they were, of an indeterminate colour, hidden beneath a frown of reflective brows; brooding eyes, suggestive of a knowledge of things that other sober citizens did not know.

The other man who stared out of the other window was younger, bigger in every way; an immense young fellow who carried in his big shoulders and clean complexion every mark of having devoted more of his college years to study of football rather than of medicine. This one grunted an ejaculation.

'I'll bet a dollar this is a patient for you.'

Dr. Muncing came over to the other window. 'I don't bet dollars with Dr. James Terry. Gambling seems to have been one of the few things you did really well at Johns College. The fellow does look plentifully frightened, at that.'

The man in question was hurrying down the street, looking anxiously at the house numbers; bent over, huddled in a raincoat, he read the numbers furtively, as though reluctant to turn his head out of the protection of his up-turned collar. He uttered a glad cry as he saw the plate of Dr. Muncing, Exorcist, and, letting the gate slam, he stumbled up the path to the door.

Dr Muncing met the man personally, led him to a comfortable chair, mixed a stimulant for him, offered him a cigarette. Calm, methodical, matter-of-fact, this was his 'bedside manner' with such cases. Forcefully he compelled the impression that, whatever might be the trouble, it was nothing that could not be cured. He stood waiting for an explanation. The man stammered an incoherent jumble of nothings.

'I—Doctor, I don't know how—I can't tell you what it is, but the Reverend Mr. Hendryx sent me to you. Yet I don't know what to tell you; there's nothing to describe.'

'Well,' said the doctor judicially, 'that is already interesting. If there's nothing and if the Reverend Mr. Hendryx feels that he can't pray it away, we probably have something that we can get hold of.'

His manner was dominant and cheerful, he radiated confidence. His bulky young assistant had been chosen for just that purpose also, to assist in putting over the impression of power, of force to deal with queer and horrible things that could not be sanely described.

The man began to respond to that atmosphere. He got a grip on himself and began to speak more coherently.

'Doctor, I don't know what to tell you. There have been no—spooks, or anything of that sort. We've seen nothing; heard nothing. It's only a feeling. I—you'll laugh at me,

Doctor, but—it's just a something in the dark that brings a feeling of awful fear; and I know that it will catch me. Last night—my God, last night it almost touched me.'

'I never laugh,' said Dr. Muncing seriously, 'until I have laid my ghost. For some ghosts are horribly real. Tell me something about yourself, your family, your home and so on. And as to your fears, whatever they are, please don't try to conceal them from me.'

A baffled expression came over the man's face. 'There's nothing to tell, Doctor; nothing that's different to anybody else. I don't know what could bring this frightful thing about us. I—my name is Jarrett—I sell real estate up in the Catskills. I have a little place a hundred feet off the paved state road, two miles from the village. There's nothing old or dilapidated about the house; there's modem plumbing, electric lights, and so on. No old graveyards anywhere in the neighbourhood. Not a single thing to bring this horror; and yet—I tell you, Doctor, there's something frightful in the dark that we can feel.'

'Hm-m!' The doctor pursed his lips and walked a short beat, his hands deep in his pockets. 'A new house; no old associations. Begins to sound like an elemental, only how would such a thing have gotten loose? Or it might be a malignant geoplasm, but—Tell me about your family, Mr. Jarrett.'

There's only four of us,. Doctor. There's my wife's brother, who's an invalid; and . . .'

'Ah-h!' A quick breath came from the doctor. 'So there's a sick man, yes? What is his trouble?'

'His lungs are affected. He was advised to come to us for the mountain air; and he was getting very much better; but recently he's very much worse again. We've been thinking that perhaps this constant terror has been too much for him.'

'Hm-m, yes, indeed.' The doctor strode his quick beat back and forth; his indeterminate eyes were distinctly steel grey just now. 'Yes, yes, the terror, and the sick man who grows worse. Quite so. Who else, Mr. Jarrett? What else have you that might attract a visophaging entity?'

'A viso-what? Good God, Doctor, we haven't anything to attract anything. Besides my wife's brother there's only my son, ten years of age, and my wife. She gets it worse than any of us; she says she has even seen—but I think there's a lot of blarney in all that.' The man contrived a sick smile. 'You know how women are, Doctor; she says she has seen shapes—formless things in the dark. She likes to think she is psychic, and she is always seeing things that nobody else knows anything about.'

'Oh, good Lord!' Dr. Muncing groaned and his face was serious. 'Verily do fools rush in. All the requirements for piercing the veil. Heavens, what idiots people can be.'

Suddenly he shot an accusing finger at Mr. Jarrett. 'I suppose she makes you sit round table with her, and all that sort of stuff.'

'Yes, Doctor, she does. Raps and spelt-out messages, and so on.'

'Good Lord!' The doctor walked angrily back and forth. 'Fools by the silly thousand play with this kind of fire, and this time these poor simpletons have broken in on something.'

He whirled on the frightened relator with accusing finger, laying down the law.

'Mr. Jarrett, your foolish wife doesn't know what she has done. I myself don't know what she has turned loose or what this thing might develop into. We may be able to stop it. It may escape and grow into a world menace. I tell you we humans don't begin to know what forces exist on the other side of that thin dividing line that we don't begin to understand. The only thing to do now is to come with you immediately to your home; and we must try and find out what this thing is that has broken through and whether we can stop it.'

The Jarrett house turned out exactly as described. Modern and commonplace in every way; situated in an acre of garden and shrubbery on a sunlit slope of the Catskill Mountains.

The other houses of the straggly little village were much the same, quiet residences of normal people who preferred to retire a little beyond the noise and activity of the summer resort of Pine Bend about two miles down the state road.

The Jarrett family fitted exactly into their locale. Well meaning, hospitable rural non-entities. The lady who was psychic was over-plump and short of breath at that elevation; the son, a gangling schoolboy, evinced the shy aloofness of a country youth before strangers; the sick man, thin and drawn, with an irritable cough, showed the unnatural flush of colour on his cheeks that marked his disease.

It required very much less than Dr. Muncing's keenness to see that all of these people were in a condition of nervous tension that in itself was proof of something that had made quite an extraordinary effect on their unimaginative minds.

Dilated eyes, tremulous limbs, backward looks; all these things showed that something had brought this unfortunate family to the verge of a panic that reached the very limits of their control.

The doctor was an adept at dispelling that sort of jumpiness. Such a mental condition was the worst possible for combating 'influences,' whatever they might be. He acknowledged his introductions with easy confidence, and then he held up his hand.

'No, no, nix on that. Give me a chance to breathe. D'you

want to ruin my appetite with horrors? Let's eat first and then you can spread yourselves out on the story. No ghost likes a full stomach.'

He was purposely slangy. The immediate effect was that his hosts experienced a measure of relief. The man radiated such an impression of knowledge, of confidence, of power.

The meal, however, was at best a lugubrious one. Conversation had to be forced to dwell on ordinary subjects. The wife evinced a painful disinclination to go into the kitchen. 'Our cook left us two days ago,' she explained. The boy was silent and frightened. The sick man said little, and coughed a dry, petulant bark at intervals.

The doctor, engrossed in his plate, chattered gaily about nothing; but all the time he was watching the invalid like a hawk. James Terry did his best to distract attention from the expert's scrutiny of everybody and everything in the room. By the time the meal was over the doctor had formed his opinion about the various characteristics and idiosyncrasies of his hosts, and he dominated the company with his expansive cheerfulness.

'Well, now, let's get one of those satisfying smokes in the jimmy pipe, and you can tell me all about it. You'—selecting the lady—'you tell me. I'm sure you'll give the best account.'

The lady, flustered and frightened, was able to add very

little to what her husband had already described. There was nothing to add. A baffling nothingness enshrouded the whole situation; but it was a nothingness that was full of an unnamable fear—a feeling of terror enhanced by the 'shapes' of the wife's psychic imaginings. A nameless nothing to be combated.

The doctor shrugged with impatience. He had met with just such conditions before: the inability of people to describe their ghostly happenings with coherence. He decided on a bold experiment.

'My dear lady,' he said, devoting his attention to the psychic one, 'it is difficult to exorcise a mere feeling until we know something about the cause of it. Now I'll tell you what we ought to do. When you sit at your table for your little seances you get raps and so on, don't you? And you spell out messages from your "spirit friends," isn't it? And you'd like to go into a trance and let your "guides" control you; only you are a little nervous about it; and all that kind of stuff, no?'

'Why, yes, Doctor, that is just about what happens, but how should you know all that?'

'Hm,' grunted the doctor dryly. 'You are not alone in your foolishness, my dear lady; there are many thousands in the United States who take similar chances. They look upon psychic exploration as a parlour game. But now what I want to suggest is, let's have one of your little seances now. And you will go into a trance this time and perhaps you—I mean your guides—will tell us something. In the trance condition, which after all is a. form of hypnosis—though we do not know whether the state is auto-induced or whether it is due to the suggestion of an outside influence—in this hypnotic condition the subconscious reflexes are sensitive to influences that the more material conscious mind cannot receive.'

Mrs. Jarrett's plump hand fluttered to her breast. This was so sudden; and she had really been a little bit afraid of her seances since this terror came into the house. But the doctor was already arranging the little round table and the chairs.

Without looking round, he said, 'You need not be at all nervous this time. And I want your brother particularly to stay in the room, though not necessarily at the table. Jimmy, you sit aside and steno whatever comes through, will you.' And in a quiet aside to his friend, he added, 'Sit near the switch, and if I holler, throw on the lights instantly and see that the sick man gets a stimulant. I may be busy.'

Under the doctor's experienced direction everything was soon ready. Just the four sat at the table, the Jarrett family and the doctor. The sick brother sat tucked in an armchair by the window and Jimmy Terry near the light switch at the door.

Once more the doctor cautioned the brawny Terry, "Watch this carefully, Jimmy. I'm putting the sick man's life into your hands. If you feel anything, if you sense anything, if you *think* anything near him, snap on the lights. Don't ask anything. Act. Ready? All right then, black out.'

With the click of the switch the room was in darkness through which came only the petulant cough of the sick man. As the eyes accustomed themselves to the gloom there was sufficient glow from the moonlight outside to distinguish the dim outlines of figures.

'This is what you usually do, isn't it?' asked the doctor. 'Hands on the table and little fingers touching?' And without waiting for the reply of which he seemed to be so sure, he continued, 'All the usual stuff, I see. But now, Mrs. Jarrett, I'm going to lay my hands over yours and you will go into a trance. So. Quiet and easy now. Let yourself go.'

In a surprisingly short space of time the table shivered with that peculiar inward tremor so familiar to all dabblers in the psychic. Shortly thereafter' it heaved slowly up and descended with a vast deliberation. There was a moment's stillness fraught with effort; then a rhythmic tap-tap-tap of one leg.

'Now,' said the doctor authoritatively. 'You will go into a trance, Mrs. Jarrett. Softly, easily. Let go. You're going into a trance. Going . . . going . . .' His voice was soothingly commanding.

Mrs. Jarrett moaned, her limbs jerked, she stretched as if

in pain; then with a sigh she became inert.

'Watch out, Jimmy,' the doctor warned in a low voice. Then to the woman: 'Speak. Where are you? What do you see?'

The plump, limp bulk moaned again. The lips moved; inarticulate sounds proceeded from them, the fragments of unformed words; then a quivering sigh and silence. The doctor took occasion to lean first to one side and then to the other to listen to the breathing of Mr. Jarrett and the boy. Both were a little faster than normal; under the circumstances, not strange. With startling suddenness words cut the dark, clear and strong.

'I am in a place full of mist, I don't know where. Grey mist.' A laboured silence. Then: 'I am at the edge of something; something deep, dark.' A pause. 'Before me is a curtain, dim and misty—no—it seems—I think—no, it is the mist that is the curtain. There are dim things moving beyond the curtain.'

'Ha!' An exclamation of satisfaction from the doctor.

'I can't make them out. They are not animals; not people. They are dark things. Just—shapes.'

'Good God, that's what she said before!' The awed gasp was Mr. Jarrett's.

The sick man coughed gratingly.

'The shapes move, they twine and roll and swell up. They

bulge up against the curtain as if to push through. It is dark; too dark on that side to see. I am afraid if one might push through . . .'

Suddenly the boy whimpered, 'I don't like this. It's cold, an' I'm scared.'

The doctor could hear the hard breathing of Mr. Jarrett on his left as the table trembled under his sudden shiver. The doctor himself experienced an enveloping depression, an almost physical crawling of the cold hairs up and down his spine. The sick man went into a spasm of violent coughing.

Suddenly the voice screamed, 'One of the shapes is almost—my God, it *is* through! It's on this side. I can see—oh God, save me.'

'Lights, Jimmy!' snapped the doctor. 'Look to the sick man.'

The swift flood of illumination showed Mr. Jarrett grey and beaded with perspiration; the boy in wild-eyed terror; Terry, too, big-eyed, and nervously alert. All of them had felt a sudden stifling weight of a clutching fear that seemed to hang like a destroying wave about to break.

The sick man was in paroxysm of coughing from which he passed into a swoon of exhaustion. Only the woman had remained blissfully unconscious. The voice that had spoken out of her left her untroubled. In heavy peacefulness she slumped in her trance condition.

The doctor leaped round the table to her and placed his hands over her forehead in protection from he did not know exactly what. A chill still pervaded the room; a physical sense of cold and lifting of hair. Some enormous material menace had almost been able to swoop upon a victim. Slowly, with the flashing on of the lights, the horror faded.

The doctor bent over the unconscious lady. Smoothly he began to stroke her face, away from the centre towards her temples. As he stroked he talked, softly, reassuringly.

Presently the woman shuddered, heaved ponderously. Her eyes opened blankly, without comprehension. Wonder dawned in them at the confusion.

'I must have been asleep,' she murmured; and she was able to smile sheepishly. 'Tell me, did I—did my guides speak?'

That foolish, innocent question, coming from the only one in the room who knew nothing of what had happened, served to dissipate fear more than all the doctor's reassurances. The others began to take hold of themselves. The doctor was able to turn his attention to the sick man.

'How is his pulse, Jimmy? Hm-m, weak, but still going. He's just exhausted. That thing drew an awful lot of strength out of him. It nearly slipped one over on me; I didn't think it was through into this side yet.'

To his hosts he said with impressive gravity, 'It is necessary to tell you that we are faced with a situation that is more dangerous than I had thought. There is in this thing a distinct physical danger; it has gone beyond imagination and beyond "sensing" things. We are up against a malignant entity that is capable of human contacts. We must get the patient up to bed and then I shall try to explain what this danger is.'

He took the limp form in his arms with hardly an effort and signified to Mrs. Jarrett to lead the way. To all appearances it was no more than an unusually vigorous physician putting a patient to bed. But the doctor made one or two quite extraordinary innovations.

'Fresh air to the contrary,' he said grimly. 'Windows must remain shut and bolted. Let me see: iron catches are good. And, Johnny, you just run down to the kitchen and bring me up a fire iron—a poker, tongs, anything. A stove lid lifter will do.'

The boy clung to the close edges of the group. The doctor nodded with understanding.

'Mr. Jarrett, will you go? We mustn't leave our patient until we have him properly protected."

In a few moments Mr. Jarrett returned with a plain iron kitchen poker. That was just the thing, the doctor said. He placed it on the floor close along the door jamb. He herded the others out and, coming last himself, shut the door, pausing just a moment to note that the lock was of iron, after which he followed the wondering family down to the living-room. They sat expectant, uneasy.

'Now,' the doctor began, as though delivering a lecture. 'I want you all to listen carefully, because—I must tell you this, much as I dislike to frighten you—this thing has gone so far that a single mis-step may mean a death.'

He held up his hand. 'No, don't interrupt. I'm going to try to make clear what is difficult enough anyhow; and you must all try to understand it because an error now—even a little foolishness, a moment of forgetfulness—can open the way for a tragedy; because—now let me impress you with this—the thing that you have felt is a palpable force. I can tell you what it is, but I cannot tell you how it came to break into this side. This malignant force is'—he paused to weigh his words—'an elemental. I do not know how the thing was released. Maybe you had nothing to do with it. But you, madam'—to the trembling Mrs. Jarrett—'you caused it by playing with this seance business, about the dangers of which you know nothing. Nor have you taken the trouble even to read up on the subject. You have opened the way to attract this thing to your house; you and the unfortunate, innocent sick man upstairs. You've actually invited it to live among you.'

The faces of the audience expressed only fear of the unknown; fear and a blank lack of understanding. The doctor controlled his impatience and continued his lecture.

'I can't go into the complete theory of occultism here and now; but this much you must understand,' he said, pounding his fist on his knee for emphasis; 'It is an indubitable fact, known throughout the ages of human existence, and re-established by modern research, that there exist certain vast discarnate forces alongside of us and all around us. These forces function according to certain controlling laws, just as we do. They probably know as little about our laws as we do about theirs.

'There are many kinds of these forces. Forces of a high intelligence, far superior to ours; forces of possibly less intelligence; benevolent forces; malignant ones. They are all loosely generalized as spirits: elementals, subliminals, earthbounds and so on.

'These forces are separated from us, prevented from contact, by—what shall I say? I dislike the word, evil, or curtain; or, as the Bible puts it, the great gulf. They mean nothing. The best simile is perhaps in the modern invention of the radio.

'A certain set of wavelengths, ethereal vibrations, can impinge themselves upon a corresponding instrument attuned to those vibrations. A slight variation in wavelength, and the receiving instrument is a blank; totally unaffected, though it knows that vibrations of tremendous power exist all around it. It must tune in to become receptive to another set of vibrations.

'In something after this manner these discarnate so-called spirit forces are prevented from impinging themselves upon our consciousness. Sometimes we humans, for reasons of which we are very often unaware, do something, create a condition, which tunes us in with the vibration of a certain group of discarnate forces. Then we become conscious; we establish contact; we, in common parlance, see a ghost.'

The lecturer paused. Vague understanding was apparent on the faces of his fascinated audience.

'Good! Now then—I mentioned elementals. Elementals comprise one of these groups of discarnate forces; possibly the lowest of the group and the least intelligent. They have not evolved to human, or even animal form. They are just—shapes.'

'Oh, my God!' the shuddering moan came from Mrs. Jarrett. 'The shapes that I have sensed!'

'Exactly. You have sensed such a shape. Why have you sensed it? Because somehow, somewhere, something has happened that has enabled one of these elemental entities to tune in on the vibrations of our human wavelength, to break through the veil. What was the cause or how, we have no means of knowing. What we do know about elementals, as has been fully recognized by occultists of the past ages and has been pooh-poohed only by modern materialism, is that they are, to begin with, malignant; that is, hostile to human life. Then again—now mark this well—they can manifest themselves materially to humans only by drawing the necessary force from a human source, preferably from some human in a state of low resistance; from—a sick man.'

'Oh, my—my brother?' Mrs. Jarrett gasped her realization.

The doctor nodded slowly.

'Yes, his condition of low resistance and your thoughtless reaching for a contact in your seances have invited this malignant entity to this house. That is why the sick man has taken this sudden turn for the worse. The elemental is sapping his vitality in order to manifest itself materially. So far you have only felt its malevolent presence. Should it succeed in drawing to itself sufficient force it might be capable of enormous and destructive power. No, no, don't scream now; that doesn't help. You must all get a grip on yourselves so as calmly to take the proper defensive precautions.

'Fortunately we know an antidote; or let me say rather, a deterrent. Like most occult lore, this deterrent has been known and used by all peoples even up to this age of modern scepticism. Savage people throughout the world use it; oriental peoples with a sensitivity keener than our own use it; modern white people use it, though unconsciously. The literature of magic is full of it.

21

'It is nothing more or less than iron. Cold iron. The iron nose-ring or toe-ring of the savage; the mantra loha of the Hindoos; the lucky horseshoe of your rural neighbours today. These things are not ornaments; they are amulets.

'We do not know why cold iron should act as a deterrent to certain kinds of hostile forces—call them spirits, if you like. But it is a fact known of old that a powerful antipathy exists between cold iron and certain of the lower orders of inhuman entities: doppelgangers, churels, incubi, wood runners, leperlings, and so on, and including all forms of elementals.

'So powerful is this antipathy that these hostile entities cannot approach a person or pass a passage so guarded. There are other forms of deterrents against some of the other discarnate entities: pentagons, Druid circles, etc., and even the holy water of the Church. Don't ask me why or how— perhaps it has something to do with molecular vibrations. Let us be glad, for the present, that we know of this deterrent. And let each of you go to bed now with a poker or a stove lid or whatever you fancy as an amulet, which I assure you will be ample to protect a normal healthy person who does not contrive to establish some special line of contact which may counteract the deterrent. In the case of the. sick man I have taken the extra precaution of guarding even the door.

'Now the rest of you go to bed and *stay in your rooms*. If

you're nervous, you may sleep all in one room. Dr. Terry and I will sit up and prowl around a bit. If you hear a noise it will be us doing night watchman. You can sleep in perfect security, unless you commit some piece of astounding foolishness which will open an unguarded avenue of contact. And one more thing: warn your brother, even if he should feel well enough, not in any circumstances to leave his room. Good night; and sleep well—if you can.'

Hesitant and unwilling the family went upstairs; huddled together, fearful of every new sound, every old shadow, not knowing, how this horror that had come into the house might manifest itself; hating to go, but worn out by fatigue engendered of extreme terror.

'I'll bet they sleep all in one room like sardines,' commented the doctor.

Terry caught the note of anxiety and asked, 'Was that all the straight dope? I mean about elementals and so on? And iron? Sounds kind of foolish.'

The doctor's face was sober, the irises of his indeterminate eyes so pale that they were almost invisible in the artificial light.

'You never listened to a less foolish thing, my boy. It sounds so to you only because you have been bred in the school of modern materialism. What? Is it reasonable to maintain that we have during the last thin fringe of years on humanity's history obliterated what has been known to humanity ever since the first anthropoid hid his head under his hairy arms in terror? We have but pushed these things a little farther away; we have become less sensitive than our forefathers. And, having become less sensitive, we naturally do not inadvertently tune in on any other set of vibrations; and so we proclaim loudly that no such things exist. But we are beginning to learn again; and if you have followed the trend you will surely have noticed that many of our leading men of science, of thought, of letters, have admitted their belief in things which science and religion have tried to deny.'

Terry was impressed with the truth of his friend's statement. The possibilities thus opened up made him uneasy.

'Well, er-er, this—this elemental thing,' he said uneasily, 'can it do anything?'

'It can do'—the indeterminate eyes were far-away pinpoints—'it can do anything, everything. Having once broken into our sphere, our plane, our wavelength—call it what you will—its malignant potentiality is measured only by the amount of force it can draw from its human source of supply. And remember—here is the danger of these things— the measure is not on a par ratio. It doesn't mean that such a malignant entity, drawing a few ounces of energy from a sick man, can exert only those few ounces. In some manner which we do not understand, all the discarnate intelligences know how to step-up an almost infinitesimal amount of human energy to many hundreds percent of power; as for instance the "spirits" that move heavy tables, perform levitation and so on. A malignant spirit can use that power as a deadly, destructive force.'

'But, good Lord,' burst out Terry, 'Why should the thing be malignant? Why, if it has broken through, got into tune with human vibrations, why should it want to destroy humans who have never done it any harm?'

The doctor did not reply at once. He was listening, alert and taut.

'Do these people keep a dog, do you know, Jimmy? Would that be it snuffling outside the door?'

But the noise, if there had been any, had ceased. The silence was sepulchral. The doctor relaxed and took up the last question.

'Why should it want to destroy life? That's something of a poser. I might say, how do I know? But I have a theory. Remember I said that elementals belonged to one of the least intelligent groups of discarnate entities. Now, the lower one goes in the scale of human intelligence, the more prevalent does one find the superstition that by killing one's enemy one acquires the good qualities of that enemy, his strength or his valour or his speed or something. In the lowest scale we find cannibalism, which is, as so many leading ethnologists have demonstrated, not a taste for human flesh, but a ceremony, a ritual whereby the eater absorbs the strength of the victim. And I suppose you know, incidentally, that militant modern atheists maintain that the holy communion is no other than a symbol of that very prevalent idea. An unintelligent elemental, then . . .'

The doctor suddenly gripped his friend's arm. A creak had sounded on the stairs. In the tense silence both men fancied they could detect a soft, sliding scuffle in that direction. With uncontrollable horror Terry's heart came up to his throat. In one panther bound the doctor reached the door and tore it open. Then he swore in baffled irritation.

Through the open door Terry could hear distinctly scurrying steps on the first landing. In sudden surge of horror at being left alone he leaped from his chair to follow his friend, and bumped into him at the door.

Dr. Muncing, cursing his luck in a most plebian manner, noted his expression and became immediately the scientist again.

'What's this, what's this? This won't do. Scare leaves you vulnerable. Now let me psychoanalyze you and eliminate that. Sit down and get this; it's quite simple and quite necessary before we start out chasing this thing. You feel afraid for two reasons. The first is psychological. Our forebears knew that certain aspects of the supernatural were genuinely fearsome. Unable to differentiate the superstition grew amongst the laity that all aspects were to be feared, just as most people fear all snakes, though only six per cent of them are poisonous. You have inherited both fear and superstition. Secondly, in this particular case, you sense the hostility of this thing and its potential power for destruction. Therefore, you are afraid.'

Under the doctor's cold logic, his friend was able to regain at least a grip on his emotions. With a smile he said, 'That's pretty thin comfort when even you admit its power for destruction.'

'*Potential*, I said. Don't forget, potential,' urged the doctor. 'It's power is capable of becoming enormous. Up to the present it has not been able to absorb very much energy. It evaded us just now instead of attacking us, and we have shut off its source of supply. Remember, too, its manifestation of itself must be physical. It may claw your hair in the dark; perhaps push you over the banisters if it gets a chance; but it can't sear your brain and blast your soul. It has drawn to itself sufficient physical energy to make itself heard; that means to be felt, and possibly to be seen. It has materialized; it cannot suddenly fade through walls and doors.'

'To be seen?' said Terry in awe-struck tones. 'Good gosh, what does a tangible hate look like?'

The doctor nodded. 'Well put, Jimmy; very well expressed. A tangible hate is just what this thing is. And since it is inherently a formless entity, a shape in the dark, manifesting itself by drawing upon human energy, it will probably look like some gross distortion of human form. Just malignant eyes, maybe, or clutching hands; or perhaps something more complete. Its object will be to skulk about the house seeking for an opening to absorb more energy to itself. Ours must be to rout it out.'

Mentally Terry was convinced. He could not fail to be, after that lucid exposition of exactly what they were up against. But physically the fine hair still rose on his spine. Shapeless things that could hate and could lurk in dark corners to trip one up on the stairs were sufficient reason for the very acme of human fear. However, he stood up. 'I'm with you,' he said shortly. 'Go ahead.'

The doctor held out his hand. 'Stout fellow. I knew you would, of course; and I brought this along for you as being quite the best weapon for this sort of a job. A blackjack in hand is a strong psychological bracer, and it has the virtue of being iron.'

Terry took the weighty little thing with a feeling of vast security, which was instantly dispelled by the doctor's next words.

'I suppose,' said Terry. 'That on account of the iron the

thing can't approach one.'

'Don't fool yourself,' said the other. 'Iron is a deterrent. Not an absolute talisman in every case. We are going after this thing; we are *inviting* contact. Just as a savage dog may attack a man who is going after it with a club, so our desperate elemental, if it sees a chance, may—well, I don't know what it can do yet. Stick close, that's all.'

Together the two men went up the stairs and stood in the upper hall. Four bedrooms and a bathroom opened off this. Two of the rooms they knew to be occupied. The other doors stood similarly closed.

'We've got to try the rooms,' the doctor whispered. 'It probably can, if necessary, open an unlocked door, though I doubt whether it would turn an iron key.'

Firmly, without hesitation, he opened one of the doors and stepped into the room. The doctor switched on the light. Nothing was to be seen, nothing heard, nothing felt.

'We'd sense it if it were here,' said the doctor as coolly as though hunting for nothing more tangible than an odour of escaping gas. 'It must be in the other empty room. Come on.'

He threw the door of that room wide open and stood, shoulder-to-shoulder with Terry, on the threshold. But there was nothing; no sound; no sensation.

'Queer,' muttered the doctor. 'It came up the stairs. It

would hardly go into the bathroom, with an iron tub in it—though God knows, maybe cast iron molecules don't repel like hand-wrought metal.'

The bathroom drew blank. The two men looked at each other, and now Terry was able to grin. This matter of hunting for a presence that evaded them was not nearly so fearsome as his imagination had conjured up. The doctor's eyes narrowed to slits as he stood in thought.

'Another example,' he murmured, 'of the many truths in the Bible about the occult. Face the devil and he will fly from you, eh? I wonder where the devil this devil can be?'

As though in immediate answer came the rasping sounds of a dry grating cough.

Instinctively both men's heads flew round to face the sick man's door. But that remained undisturbed; the patient seemed to be sleeping soundly. Suddenly the doctor gripped his friend's arm and pointed—up to the ceiling.

'From the attic. See that trapdoor. It has taken on the cough with the vital energy it has been drawing from the sick man. I guess there'll be no lights up there. I'll go and get my flashlight. You stay here and guard the stairs. Then you can give me a boost up.'

The doctor was becoming more incredible every minute.

'You mean to say you propose to stick your head up through there?'

The doctor nodded soberly; his eyes were now black beads.

'It's quite necessary. You see, we've got to chase this thing out of the house while it is still weak, and then protect all entrances. Then, if it cannot quickly establish a contact with some other sick and non-resistant source of energy, it must go back to where it came from. Without a constant replenishment of human energy it can't keep up the human vibrations. That's the importance of shutting it out while it is still too weak to break through anybody else's resistance somewhere else. It's quite simple, isn't it? You sit tight and play cat over the mouse hole. I'll be right up again.'

Cat-like himself, the doctor ran down the steps. Terry felt chilled despite the fact that the hall was well lighted and he was armed. But that black square up there—if any cover belonged over it, it had been removed. The hole gaped dark, forbidding; and somewhere beyond it in the misty gloom a formless thing coughed consumptively. Terry, gazing at the hole in fascinated terror, imagined for himself a sudden framing of baleful eyes, a reaching down of a long taloned claw.

It grew to a horror, staring at that black opening, as into an evil world beyond. The effort of concentration became intolerable. Terry felt that he could not for the life of him hold his stare; he had to relieve himself of that tension or he would scream. He felt that cry welling up in his throat and the chill rising of hair on his scalp. He let his eyes drop and took a long breath to recover the control that was slipping from him.

There came a sharp click from the direction of the electric switch, and the hall was in sudden blackness.

Terry stood frozen, the cry choked in his throat. He could not tell how long he remained transfixed. An age passed in motionless fear of he did not know what. What had turned off the lights?

In the blackness a board creaked with awful deliberation. Terry could not tell where. His faculties refused to register. Only his wretched imagination—or was it his imagination?— conjured up a shadow, darker than the dark, poised on one grotesque foot like some monstrous misshapen carrion bird, watching him with a fell intentness. His pulse hammered at his temples for what seemed an eternity of horror. He computed time later by the fact that his eyes were becoming accustomed to the dim glow that came from the light downstairs.

Another board creaked, and now Terry felt his knees growing limp. But that was the doctor's firm step on the lower stairs. Terry's knees stiffened and he began to be able to breathe once more.

The shadow seemed to know that Dr. Muncing was

returning, too. Terry was aware of a rush, of a dimly monstrous density of blackness that launched itself at him. He was hurled numbingly against the wall by a muffling air-cushion sort of impact. Helplessly dazed, smothered, he did not know how to resist, to defend himself. He was lost. And then the glutinous pressure recoiled, foiled. He could almost hear the baffled hate that withdrew from him and hurtled down the stairs.

His senses registered the fact that without his own volition he shouted, 'Look out!' and that there was a commotion somewhere below. He heard a stamping of feet and a surge of wind as though a window had been blasted open; and the next thing was the doctor's inquiry, 'Are you hurt?' and the beam of a flashlight racing up the steps.

He was not hurt; miraculously, it seemed to him, for the annihilating malevolence of that formless creature had appeared to be a vast force. But the doctor dressed him down severely.

'You lost your nerve, in spite of all that I explained to you. You let it influence your mind to fear and so played right into its hands. You laid yourself open to attack as smoothly as though you were Mrs. Jarrett herself. But out of that very evil we can draw the good of exemplary proof.

'You were helpless; paralyzed. And yet the thing drew off. Why? Because you had your iron blackjack in your hand.

If it had known you had that defence it would never have attacked you, or it would have influenced you to put the iron down first. Knowing now that you have it, it will not, in its present condition of weakness, attack you again. So stick that in your hat and don't get panicky again. But we've got to keep after it. If we can keep it out of the house; if we can continue so to guard the sick man that the thing cannot draw any further energy from him its power to manifest itself must dwindle. We shall starve it out. And the more we can starve it, the less power will it have to break through the resistance of a new victim.'

'Come on, then,' said Terry.

'Good man,' approved the doctor. 'Come ahead. It went through the living-room window; that was the only one open. But, why, I ask myself. Why did it go out? That was just what we wanted it to do. I wonder whether it is up to some devilish trick. The thing can think with a certain animal cunning. We must shut and lock the living-room window and go out at the door. What trick has that thing in store, I wonder? What damnable trick?'

'How are we going to find an abstract hate in this maze of shadows?' Terry wanted to know.

'It is more than abstract,' said the doctor seriously. 'Having broken into our plane of existence, this thing has achieved, as you have already felt, a certain state of semi-materialization. A ponderable substance has formed round the nucleus of malignant intelligence. As long as it can draw upon human energy from its victim, that material substance will remain. In moving from place to place, it must make a certain amount of noise. And, drawing its physical energy from this particular sick man, it must cough as he does. In a good light, even in this bright moonlight, it will be, to a certain extent, visible.'

But no rustlings and scurryings fled before their flashlights amongst the ornamental evergreens; no furtive shadow flitted across moonlight patches; no sense of hate hung in the darkest corners.

'I hope to God it didn't give us the slip and sneak in again before we got the entries fixed. But no, I'm sure it wasn't in the house. I wish I could guess what tricks it's up to.' The doctor was more worried than he cared to let his friend see. He was convinced that leaving the house had been a deliberate move on the thing's part and he wished that he might fathom whatever cunning purpose lay back of that move.

All of a sudden the sound of footsteps impinged upon their ears; faint shuffling. Both men tensed to listen, and they could hear the steps coming nearer. The doctor shook his head.

'It's just some countryman trudging home along the road.

If he sees us with flashlights at this hour he'll raise a howl of burglars, no doubt.'

The footsteps approached ploddingly behind the fence, one of those nine-foot high ornamental screens made of split chestnut saplings that are so prevalent around country houses. Presently the dark figure of the man—Terry was quite relieved to see that it was a man—passed before the open gate, and the footsteps trudged on behind the tall barrier.

Fifty feet, a hundred feet; the crunch of heavy nailed boots was growing fainter. Then something rustled amongst the bushes. Terry caught at the doctor's sleeve. 'There! My God! There again!'

A crouching something ran with incredible speed along this side of the fence after the unsuspecting footsteps of the other. In the patches of moonlight between black shadows it was easily distinguishable. It came abreast with the retreating footsteps and suddenly it jumped. Without preparation or take-off, apparently without effort, the swiftly scuttling thing shot itself into the air.

Both men saw a ragged-edged form, as that of an incredibly tall and thin man with an abnormally tiny head, clear the nine-foot fence with bony knees drawn high and attenuated ape arms flung wide; an opium eater's nightmare silhouetted against the dim sky. And then it was gone.

In the instant that they stood rooted to the spot, a shriek of inarticulate terror rose from the road. There was a spurt of flying gravel, a mad plunging of racing footsteps, more shrieks, the last rising to the high-pitched falsetto of the acme of fear. Then a lurching fall and an awful silence.

'Good God!' The doctor was racing for the gate, Terry after him. A hundred feet down the road a dark mass huddled on the ground; there was not a sign of anything else. The misshapen shadow had vanished. The man on the ground rolled limp, giving vent to great gulping moans. The doctor lifted his shoulders against his own knee.

'Keep a look-out, Jimmy,' he warned. His deft hands were exploring for a hurt or wound, while his rapid fire of comments gave voice to his findings. 'What damned luck! Still, I don't see what it could have done to a sturdy lout like this. How could we have guarded against this sort of a mischance? Though it just couldn't have crashed into this fellow's vitality so suddenly; there doesn't seem to be anything wrong, anyhow. I guess he's more scared than hurt.'

The moaning hulk of a man squirmed and opened his eyes. Feeling himself in the grip of hands, he let out another fearful yell and struggled in a frenzy to escape.

'Easy, brother, easy,' the doctor said soothingly. 'You're all right. Get a hold of yourself.'

The man shuddered convulsively. Words babbled from his

sagging lips. 'It-it-its ha-hand! Oh, G—God—over my face. A h-hand like an eel—a dead ee-eel. Ee-ee!'

He went off into a high-pitched hysteria again.

There was a sound of windows opening up at the house and a confused murmur of anxious voices; then a hail.

'What is it? Who's there? What's the matter?'

'Lord help the fools!' The doctor dropped the man cold in the road and sprang across to the other side from where he could look over the high fence and see the square of patches of light from the windows high up on their little hill.

'Back!' he screamed. 'Get back! For God's sake, shut those windows!' He waved his hands and jumped down in an agony of apprehension. 'What?' The fatuous query floated down to him. 'What's that you say?'

Another square of light suddenly sprang out of the looming mass, from the sick man's room. Laboriously the window went up, and the sick man leaned out.

'What?' he asked, and he coughed out into the night.

'God Almighty! Come on, Jimmy! Leave that fool; he's only scared.' The doctor shouted and dashed off on the long sprint back to the gate and up the sloping shrubbery to the house that he had' thought to leave so well guarded.

'That's its trick,' he panted as he ran. 'That's why it came out. Please Providence we won't come too late. But it's got the start on us, and it can move ten times as fast.'

Together they burst through the front door, slammed it after them, and thundered up the stairs. The white, owlish faces of the Jarrett family gleamed palely at them from their door. The doctor cursed them for fools as he dashed past. He tore at the knob of the sick-room door.

The door did not budge.

Frantically he wrestled with it. It held desperately solid.

'Bolted from the inside!' The doctor screamed. 'The fool must have done it himself. Open up in there. Quick! Open for your life.'

The door remained cold and dead. Only from inside the room came the familiar hacking cough. It came in a choking fit. And then Terry's blood ebbed in a chill wave right down to his feet.

For *there were two coughs*. A ghastly chorus of rasping and retching in a hell's paroxysm.

The doctor ran back the length of the hall. Pushing off from the further wall, he dashed across and crashed his big shoulders against the door. Like petty nails the bolt screws flew and he staggered in, clutching the sagging door for support.

The room was in heavy darkness. The doctor clawed wildly along the wall for the unfamiliar light switch. Terry, at his heels, felt the wave of malevolence that met them.

The sudden light revealed to their blinking eyes the sick

man, limp, inert, lying where he had been hurled, half in and half out of the bed, twisted in a horrible paroxysm.

The window was open, as the wretched dupe had left it when he poked his foolish head out into the night to inquire about all the hubbub outside. Above the corner of the sill, hanging outside, was a horror that drew both men up short. An abnormally long angle of raggy elbow supported a smudgy, formless, yellow face of incredible evil that grinned malignant triumph out of an absurdly infantile head.

The face dropped out of sight. Only hate, like a tangible thing, pervaded the room. From twenty feet below came back to the trembling men a grating, 'Och-och-och, ha-ha-ha-heh-heh-heck, och—och.' It retreated down the shrubbery.

Dr. Muncing stood a long minute in choked silence. Then bitterly he swore. Slowly, with incisive grimness he said, 'Man's ingenuity can guard against everything except the sheer dumb stupidity of man.'

It was morning. Dr. Muncing was taking his leave. He was leaving behind him a few last words of advice. They were not gentle.

'I shall say no more about the criminal stupidity of opening your windows after my warning to you; perhaps the thing was able to influence all of you. Your brother, madam, has paid the price. Through your fault and his, there is now loose, somewhere in our world, an elemental entity, malignant and having sufficient human energy to continue. Where or how, I cannot say. It may turn up in the next town, it may do so in China; or something may happen to dissipate it.

'As far as you are concerned it is through. It has tapped this source of energy and has gone on. It will not come back, unless you, madam, go out of your way deliberately to attract it by fooling with these silly seances before you have learned a lot more about them than you know now.'

Mrs. Jarrett was penitent and very wholesomely frightened, besides. She would never play with fire again, she vowed; she would have nothing at all to do with it ever again; she would be glad if the doctor would take away her ouija board and her planchette and all her notebooks; everything. She was afraid of them; she felt that some horrible influence still attached to them.

'Notebooks?' The doctor was interested. 'You mean you took notes of the babble that came through? Let me see. Hm-m, the usual stuff; projected reversal of your own conceptions of the hereafter and how happy all your relatives are there. Ha, what's this? Numbers, numbers—twelve, twenty-four, eight—all the bad combinations of numbers. What perversity made you think only of bad numbers? Hello, hello, what—From where did you get this recurring ten, five, eight, one, fourteen? A whole page of it. And here again. And here; eighteen, one, ten? Pages and pages—and a lot of worse ones here? How did this come?'

Mrs. Jarrett was tearful and appeared somewhat hesitant.

'They just came through like that, Doctor. They kept on coming. We just wrote them down.'

The doctor was very serious. A thin whistle formed in his pursed lips. His eyes were dark pools of wonder.

'There are more things in heaven and earth—' He muttered. Then shaking off the awe that had come over him, he turned to Mrs. Jarrett.

'My dear lady,' he said. 'I apologize about those open windows. This thing was able to project its influence from even the other side of the veil. *It made you invite it.* Don't ask me to explain these mysteries. But listen to what you have been playing with.' The doctor paused to let his words soak in.

'These numbers, translated into their respective letters, are the beginning of an ancient *Hindoo Yogi spell to invoke a devil.* Merciful heaven, how many things we don't understand. So that's how it came through. And there is no Yogi spell to send it back. We shall probably meet again, that thing and I.'